WIZARDING WORLD

FRIENDSHIP WITH A PHOENIX

ANNA MARGARET YOHAN

Copyright © 2017 Anna Margaret Yohan

All rights reserved.

ISBN: 9781973343509

DEDICATION

For my parents, Benediktus and Jovita Yohan

I made this story for anyone who loves novel stories, Phoenixes, fantasies, magics, adventures, and imagining things. Happy Reading!

CONTENTS

	ACKNOWLEDGMENTS	i
1	THE NIGHT BEFORE SCHOOL	1
2	THE SCHOOL BEGINS	8
3	THE INTRODUCTION OF THE TEACHERS	19
4	THE FIRST LESSON ABOUT THE POTIONS	29
5	THE MAGIC WAND'S TRICKS	35
6	THE FLYING BROOM LESSON	41
7	THE 'HOW TO SEE YOUR FUTURE' LESSON	50
8	THE MYTH CREATURES LESSON	56
9	THE LESSON WITH PROFESSOR VICTOR	62
10	THE 'FLYBALL' GAME	68
11	THE TALKS ABOUT THE SAME DREAM	76
12	THE 'FLYBALL' MATCH	82
13	THE ATTACKS	88
14	THE FIGHTING WITH SCOBATS AND THE SECRETS	95

15	THE NEW MEMBER OF ADVENTURER TEAM	104
16	ANOTHER MYSTERY	110
17	THE FIGHTING PART 2	116
18	THE FIGHTING WITH PROFESSOR NORICKED	126
19	THE TRUTH	132
20	THE CELEBRATION AND THE QUESTIONS	138
21	THE BATTLE	144
22	THE PURE ANIMTRA	149
23	THE LAST NIGHT IN THE YEAR AND THE RETURN TO HOME	157

ACKNOWLEDGMENTS

I would like to thank all who supported me in writing and publishing this book.

CHAPTER 1
THE NIGHT BEFORE SCHOOL

Hank Witter Kenelog, a teenage boy, Phonnet the female Phoenix who was still in egg form, and Vivian Netter, a teenage girl, were sitting on Hank's treehouse, watching sunset.

They were neighbors, and they were waiting the day that Hank's Phoenix egg would be hatched, becoming Phonnet.

They had received a mail from Frangs, a poison fang bird sized a duck, the mail delivery bird. Every family received a letter with a name of their kids on it.

Hank was from the Kenelog family and Vivian was from the Netter family, and they would enter the popular wizarding school, School of Wizardry, the school of magic. The school only accept students aged 12 up to 14 to study the first level of wizardry.

"Wow! In our twelfth age, I mean, this year, we will...."

"Start our wizarding school!", continued Vivian before Hank finished.

"I wonder what will it be?", said Hank with his dreamy eyes set.

Hank was a chubby boy with a shining, black wizard robe, brown shining hair, and light-brown skin. Vivian was a slim girl with brown square glasses, long wavy hair, shining purple wizard robe, and light-brown skin.

"How is our school? Are there mysteries?", asked Vivian.

"Why do you ask me? I said I didn't know for several times. Just see tomorrow Vivian!", answered Hank.

"Oh, ok, sorry. I am just too eager", said Vivian slowly.

"Vivian! Come back! Eat your dinner!", Vivian's mother's voice heard from beside Hank's house.

"Well, see you tomorrow with Phonnet. Eat your dinner!", said Hank.

"Thanks Hank, I just didn't notice that it's night now. Just come down and eat your dinner too, Hank! Don't be too late!", answered Vivian.

"Ok Vivian, see you tomorrow!"

They climbed down the tree with the egg of Phonnet the Phoenix in Hank's pocket. Vivian ran to her family's house, and Hank went to his house.

Hank and Vivian ate their dinner. Before that, they took a bath, and talked some time again from their bedroom window, and they ate their dinner.

After dinner, they went to brush their teeth, and to their bedroom, talked some again about 10 minutes from their bedroom window, and tried to sleep below the twinkling stars and the half-moon.

Hank and Vivian went to look their magic stuffs thrown near their bedroom window from their bed, and couldn't fall asleep, because, they wanted to see their new school tomorrow and very eager how it looked like.

In their head, they only knew that they would live in school except for the summer holiday. They wanted more adventures and experiences in their school, so … they couldn't sleep until the midnight. When another day came, they fell asleep with a very beautiful dream about their adventures.

CHAPTER 2

THE SCHOOL BEGINS

Hank and Vivian woke up in 5 o'clock in the morning. Their mom and dad made sure everything was prepared while Hank and Vivian helped them prepare themselves.

"Magic wand, flying broom, cauldron…", muttered Vivian's dad.

"All set", yelled Hank's mom to Hank.

At 6 o'clock, they had prepared everything and Hank, together with Vivian, kissed their mom and dad, then went to the train station to their school: School of Wizardry.

"Whew, what a luck we arrived here at 6:05 morning", said Hank, panting.

"Put your trunks here! Put your trunks here!", shrieked a man with high voice.

"Let's go there to put our trunk and then go in to the train!", said Vivian.

They put their trunk there and went into the train.

"I...feel Phonnet the Phoenix ...hatched or the worst, cracked, Vivian", said Hank slowly, scared if the egg was cracked, not hatched.

"Get the egg out of your pocket, Hank", said Vivian with a sweaty face. *"There is none of the egg!"*, said Hank panic.

"What! Just take everything out of your pocket!", yelled Vivian to Hank, a bit afraid too.

Then, the train moved slowly to fast.
"Oh no! How about my egg? The train is moving!", whispered Hank dramatically.

"What is the red-grey thing that you get out from your pocket?", asked Vivian.

"Looks like a…oh my!", Vivian stopped.

"My Phonnet!", shrieked Hank happily.

Hank hurried up kissing Phonnet the Phoenix chick and put her again into his pocket. The train moved very fast and two hours later, the train stopped at the School of Wizardry train station. Hank and Vivian went in to the school that has magical gate guarded by griffins. They saw a large garden full of magics. There were flying candles, the teachers' bedrooms, the teachers' office, and many more such as the Feast Place and the Big Classrooms.

"Wow, wow, wow!. More than just a school!", said Vivian dreamily.

"Look! There are our trunks put in front of a place named...Grouping Station?", Hank asked.

"Everybody pick their trunk there...So, let's pick our trunk and go to a house to stay!", said Vivian happily.

They picked their trunks and went to a house near the teachers' bedrooms. When they got in, the brooms were still cleaning the floor themselves. When the brooms swept the floor, the floor would be magically cleaned.

They sat on a sofa while Hank, Vivian, and everybody being served with welcome drink and a slice of garlic bread.

"Hank! Let's just feed Phonnet with the leaves from that tree while the brooms are still cleaning!", said Vivian.

"Great idea", answered Hank and he went out of the house, picked some leaves from the short tree while Vivian played with Phonnet.

"Here we are", said Hank, panting.

"Eat this, Phonnet!", said Vivian softly.

Phonnet ate the leaves so fast and when the leaves had gone to Phonnet's little stomach, she was full.

A teacher came in and said, *"Go to the Grouping Station please"*.

Hank and Vivian hurried go to the Grouping Station and when they came in, the headmistress said, *"Please choose one person to your team with his or her pet and after that, stay on your position".*

The silent Grouping Station became very annoying when the students hurried up searching for a friend.

Hank, Vivian, and Phonnet in Hank's pocket, stayed on their position like frozen man until a teacher came to their standing area and said, *"What are you two doing, standing here like frozen men?"*

"We've finished", answered Hank and Vivian both together.

"Well, okay then, let's go up there, to the place for the Great Ball", continued the teacher.

"What is the Great Ball?", asked Hank.

"I...", answered Vivian, stopped, because they already reached the stairs to go to the Great Ball.

The Great Ball was tiny, like the golf ball.

"I want you to put your hands here, at the Great Ball, except your pet. Hear what the Great Ball say in your head.

1…2…3…! *Your hands!"*, continued the teacher.

Hank and Vivian put their hands on the 'Great Ball', and heard a voice that could only be heard by themselves and the voice was secret, *"Well, the persons who touch me are Hank and Vivian, right?*

Ha! I know there are people saved by you, and healed by your team, even though you have to do the naughty things. Well…your team's name is… Adventurers!", the voice shouted very loud until everyone heard the name of Hank and Vivian's team.

"Well, congratulations! You will be the adventurers to save us, right?", asked the teacher.

"Y...yes?", answered Hank and Vivian. "Well now, go to your house. If you don't live in the same home, now as a team, you have to stay together in the same house.", said the teacher again.

"Thank you, Mam", answered Hank and Vivian, both together. They were very proud of their team's name, Adventurers.

CHAPTER 3

THE INTRODUCTION OF THE TEACHERS

The first bells rang, and it meant the breakfast. Hank and Vivian hurried going to the Feast Place.

"Is this the Feast Place, the outdoor place to eat?", asked Hank.

"Just believe what you see!", said Vivivan hungrily, while her tongue wiped her lip.

When every team came to the 'Feast Place', the foods already served. They just needed to take the food.

"I will get the garlic bread, Hank. See you there!", said Vivian, pointed to a little table that was empty.

Hank got the bread for the breakfast while Vivian the garlic bread.

"This food is yummy even though it is only a bread!", said Hank.

"This is good", said Vivian.

After one hour, the bells rang again and it meant the first lesson. When they got to the Big Classroom, all the teachers were there, waiting for the students. After all the students got in, the teachers introduced themselves,

"Hello all, I am Professor Ganag, the headmistress. My complete name is Dalla Haryta Ganag. I teach the potions. For other information, I will tell you at the lesson. Thank You", said Professor Ganag introducing herself.

Professor Ganag was a tall woman with long curly hair, covered in shining purple wizard robe, brown skin, and with the headmistress' pointed witch hat. Came the vice of the headmistress.

"Hello! My name is Martin McGall. You can call me Professor McGall. I like to teach you about the magic wand. Well, happy learning!", said Professor McGall.

Professor McGall was a chubby person with a circle brown glasses, hair straight backwards, emerald green wizard robe, and light-brown skin.

"Well hello, there!", said a short teacher, "I am Miss Miserandusy. My *complete name is Agatha Miserandusy. I teach you on the very impressive lesson…the flying broom! Well, it's…just happy to see you all…happy day!"*, she finished the last sentence with some sort of the happy tears and sobs, then she wiped (over acting).

Well…Miss Miserandusy was just a short woman with a nasty look on her face while she's smiling (like a kind of *half* painfully smiling that was very nasty), with an ugly red robe, pale skin, untidy hair, too small white glasses for her eyes, and no shoes at all.

"Take your attention again please", said a male teacher with small eyes, clapping his hands, *"I am here to teach you how to see your future...and...blah blah blah" "Sounds boring? I hear the nonsense of his talks here. I think this lesson will be no function at all. It's hurt, right? If you have to fail in your school?"*, asked Hank with his hands held up his chin on the table.

"I think no", answered Vivian excitedly.

"So...you want to learn about nonsense?", asked Hank furiously.

"I think that again twice and I think you are right", answered Vivian with disgust on her face because the look of the teacher that named Professor Talno Noricked, (he insisted to be called Professor Noricked), while the Professor talking nonsense about…15 minutes.

He was wearing slimy shoes, robes, socks, with slimes on his face, on his very short hair, and he got pale skin.

"Thank you", the last word from Professor Noricked after 15 minutes, and the other teachers who hadn't introduced themselves had a

disgusting expression on their face too.

"Ehm, well, everyone, I am Miss Dane, and my complete name is Velvety Dane", said a good-looking woman, and she was speaking with angry look to Professor Noricked.

"I teach about the Beasts, Fantastic Creature, called Mythical Creatures. Well, have fun!".

Miss Dane was a pretty woman with curly hair, white robe, and light-brown skin.

"Ehm...I think...she looks good, yeah?", asked Hank.

"Don't talk that thing Hank...just focused!", answered Vivian with anger on her face.

The next teacher came and the he was the last.

"Hello everybodeh'! Me'h is Professor Victor. Me'h teaches yuh' about how to defence yuh'selves from the darkness of the magics. Yuh' will enjoy thihs 'lesson. Thank yuh'."

Professor Victor was a very tall teacher with a pointed hat, chocolate colored robe, very pale skin, narrowed eyes, and the long untidy hair and beard. He had a very kind face and seemed to be the friendliest teacher to all. Seemed if he was angry, he would be exploded, but, he's very kind.

"The honor of the year can be received by a team that has the biggest point number. The honor is the badge of 'The Champion of the School'.", continued Professor Ganag.

CHAPTER 4

THE FIRST LESSON ABOUT THE POTIONS

All the teachers except Professor Ganag were leaving the class, and the students got a map for each team from her, map about the school.

"Chop chop! Get your cauldron here, the cleaning service has taken your cauldrons and put them here", said Professor Ganag while she pointed to the cauldrons.

"Let's focus to the Potions lesson ok?", said Professor Ganag while the students picked their cauldron.

They learnt the 'turn into animal potion', and how to use it just drank one gulp of the potion and mention the animal you wanted to turn into.

"Ok! Let's start! First! The water to add! 1 glass of water! Second! The green water! 1 glass too! Third! Take your *magic wand and tap it to the cauldron that contains the water and green water! To change it to potion, say 'animapotion'! That's it!"*, said Professor Ganag while the teams followed her instruction.

Professor Ganag reminded them how to make the 'Turn into Animal Potion'. Hank and Vivian were the first who did it and they had to drink it now. Vivian wanted to be a cat while Hank would be an eagle.

"Well, Hank and Vivian from Adventurer Team were done now and turned into a cat and an eagle. This potion's effect stays forever until you say

in your brain 'Turningwizz!'," said Professor Ganag.

Hank, (who was an eagle), was now soaring through the air, circling the class, while Vivian, (who was now a cat), was running to Professor Ganag and circling Professor Ganag's feet while Professor Ganag smiled to Hank and Vivian. Hank and Vivian went back to their seat and said *'Turningwizz'* in their brain, and they became Hank and Vivian again, sitting on their seat, with Phonnet the Phoenix still on Hank's pocket. The others were doing the same with

Hank and Vivian, and everyone was successful doing it.

"All my children, you have been successful learning to make this potion and using it. Now, we can continue our lesson to the 'Stunning potion'," and when Professor Ganag said the 'Stunning potion', the children were whimpering and whispering.

And Professor Ganag continued, *"How to make it? Follow my instructions."*

Professor Ganag said that they must add the electric from their wand to the potion after the potion was finished, and they had to use it by spreading the potion to the enemy they wanted. After one hour they learned three potions, the bells rang.

CHAPTER 5

THE MAGIC WAND'S TRICKS

Professor Ganag left the class, and Professor McGall came in and started speaking,

"Let's all take your magic wand and we will start learning with the magic words first. There are 'Shazam', 'Alakazam',

'Hocus Pocus', 'Presto', and 'Abrafonte'. Choose one for your team and this is the first spell to know, the thick bubble that protects us. Just tap it to your head two times and say your magic word, then, the protection word: 'Bobbleprotecta!'. As examples, 'Alakazam! Bobbleprotecta!'"

The students tried themselves to have the bubble of protection, and they did it as well as Professor McGall. Professor McGall was delighted to see it, but now, none of them could touch each other except with the other magic.

"Now, we will learn the spell to hit. Just for example, I, will hit the desk", said Professor McGall while his finger pointing the old desk.

"'Alakazam! 'Hiterasta!'", said Professor McGall, pointing his wand to the desk.

A solid light hit the desk and the desk broke into two.

"Well, don't try it now, it's dangerous, and let me remind you, this spell can only make things into two, but for humans and creatures, it will only be wounds to someone who hit by the spell", Professor McGall told them.

But one of the students tried to hit Phonnet, Hank's Phoenix, and Hank made the bubble of protection for Phonnet right in time, and Phonnet was saved from harm.

"Well, Harm Team will be taken 10 points! And Adventurers Team get 10 points", said Professor McGall, looked shocked.

Hank, Vivian, and Phonnet got angry with the Harm Team's joke. The Harm Team said that it was a joke for them, and they knew that Harm Team were the barbarians for them. When they learnt another magic to hit the bad wizards and things, the Harm Team were trying to hit Vivian, but the Adventurer Team got their bubble of protection. The Harm Team was taken 10 points again, and they started to envy Hank, Vivian, and Phonnet, their little Phoenix. They had to learn more about the protection spells, and Professor McGall gave them a homework each team to learn one new protective spell together with their team. They learnt more spells at that hour and they seemed to like Professor McGall because, he was very kind to them.

Hank and Vivian didn't feel when time passed quickly.

CHAPTER 6

THE FLYING BROOM LESSON

One hour passed, and they had to go to their houses to take their own magic broom, and went to the biggest park at the school to start the lesson with Miss Miserandusy. They seemed to hate this lesson, especially Hank and Vivian, because they didn't like her over acting attitude, even though it was a very helpful lesson. Phonnet and the other pets were sitting in a corner, not far from their owners, and watched their owners practicing the magic broom.

"All my children, welcome to the Flying Broom Lesson. After you masterize how to ride the flying broom, you can start to learn with me about the tricks", said Miss Miserandusy with an over acting attitude, and her nasty smile, with a nasty giggle too.

"Well, chop chop! Take your flying broom and mount it, then, say up, and you will be floating. If you want to move, just kick the air. Direct the point of your broom to anywhere you like. How to landing is just to direct the point of your broom to the land and when you near the ground, direct your broom straight again", continued Miss Miserandusy.

Now, all students were on the air now, and ready to land. Now, in 2 minutes, everybody was back to the land now, and Miss Miserandusy was sitting beneath a big tree, calling

Hank and Vivian to come there, where she was sitting.

"Why... you two have a very great skill in flying broom lesson...", said Miss Miserandusy.

"Er...", said Vivian, confused. "We...we...don't know why. Maybe it's just...it's just us!", said Hank slowly and carefully.

The teacher continued, "You two can play 'Flyball' then..."

"We? What's 'Flyball'?", asked Hank and Vivian, confused with the 'Flyball' game.

Miss Miserandusy answered both of them with her nasty smile and said,

"Wizards and witches play this wizards game and many of them enjoy it. It's a game where you have to catch a flying and tiny ball named the 'Golden Falcon', it's named like that because of its high speed. There are obstacles like the griffin and big spiders to guard the ball. Spiders guard the ball on the grounds while griffins in the air. They guard it by trying to hit you…but I can't say they guard the ball…they just feel distracted by you and try to chase you. You have to survive against the obstacles and you have to catch it before other teams that

chosen by the 'Flyball' Captain, Gerard Bugman"

"So...so.." "Follow me", said Miss Miserandusy before Vivian finished her sentence.

Before they got out of the biggest garden, the bells rang and they kept walking to the teacher's office, where seemed that all of the teachers had walked to the 'Feast Place' except a skinny and scarred man.

"Hello Bugman", said Miss Miserandusy to the skinny man.

The skinny and young man seemed like skeletons with his smooth hair and his brown skin with his yellow shining robes shining in the lights of the candles.

"Now, what team that you bring to me, Miserandusy?", asked Bugman with his smooth voice.

"I bring the Adventurer Team, Bugman, you will like them", answered Miss Miserandusy.

"Hank and Vivian?", asked Bugman while he turned his head which the

last time he spoke, his head was still looking at a paper he wrote.

"*Yes, we are*", answered Hank.

"*Let's train on the 'Flyball' park after lunch*", said Bugman while his head turned again to his paper he wrote.

Hank and Vivian became more excited than previous. They were hurried finished their lunch and went to their house before the others, while Bugman made permissions to bring them to the 'Flyball' park to Professor Noricked, the teacher of 'How to See Your Future' lesson, who refused to give permission, and Bugman came to the Adventurer Team's house to tell that they had to practice before dinner time after finished all the lessons that day.

CHAPTER 7

THE 'HOW TO SEE YOUR FUTURE' LESSON

Hank and Vivian went to the Big Classroom again with a broken heart and a very disappointed feeling. The time seemed to get past very slowly that Hank and Vivian were very disappointed for the second time because they saw the play the 'Flyball' game and they got wounds. Hank and Vivian tried not to sleep like the other students, tried not to sleep, until they got closed their eyes and…MAGICAL! The class was changed with the 'Flyball' park.

Bugman said… *"Get your broom and here's the ball. Try to catch it!"*, he finished the last sentence by throwing the 'Golden Falcon' ball up to the sky.

Hank and Vivian saw the Griffins ready to pounce on them, and now, they chased by the Griffins. They were near the ground and suddenly, giant spiders came out and...they saw the very tiny 'Golden Falcon', shining in the sun. Vivian chased the 'Golden Falcon' while Hank tried to distract them. The Griffins and the giant spiders tried to catch Vivian, who chased the ball, while Hank was soaring up and up, tried to catch up with Vivian and distracted the Griffins. One giant Griffin pounced on Hank and the smallest Griffin pounced on Vivian and then...they were...

"*HAH!*", said Hank and Vivian quietly.

The class was now very quiet, seemed that all of the students had fallen asleep. Professor Noricked was still talking about how to see the future with the other way...which sounded more boring. Yes...all the students were sleeping silently, and Professor Noricked asked them to see all their futures, but none of them tried it except Hank and Vivian with Phonnet on Vivian's desk. They had to see in 5 minutes and suddenly before they started, all the students woke up together, and the other students knew what they had to do.

"Hank…why…?" "I don't know why Vivian", Hank said before Vivian finished her sentence.

They wanted to talk about their dreams even though they didn't know their dreams were the same, but Professor Noricked seemed to be angry if they talked.

Hank said shortly, *"I think our friends seemed to hear Professor Noricked's talk in their dream. I think…Professor Noricked used spell to make them dream about him…because, I see him on the time we woke up, he muttered something looked like a spell...*", whispered Hank quietly to Vivian and she answered, "*I think so…I think…Professor Noricked used a spell to wake them up too with a wave of his wand…I see it…and of course… Professor Noricked knows that all of us has fallen asleep, and we didn't have the effects because we slept before them…right?*"

"*Right*", answered Hank quickly before Professor Noricked seemed to spy them suspiciously.

CHAPTER 8

THE MYTH CREATURES LESSON

At last, one hour passed boringly, and Miss Dane came in.

"She is really pretty", Hank said excitedly, but awakened by Vivian and Hank looked surprised.

"Do you enjoy the lesson with him?", asked Miss Dane about Professor Noricked who just got out from the class.

"No", said Vivian flatly, followed by Hank and the other students.

"Well…let's just focus to our lesson…the myth creature. We will learn the Phoenixes. Phoenix is the gentle and small creature. Its body was like a swan and it has warm body. Phoenixes can rise again from the death, and can heal

anybody with the purity of heart. When Phoenixes' pure heart meet a pure heart of anybody who wounded, the one who has a pure heart can be healed all of his or her wounds. Phoenixes can only heal a wizard. They can't heal humans. May I take your Phoenix for this lesson, Hank?", asked Miss Dane.

Hank looked very happy and surprised, then, he walked towards Miss Dane and gave Phonnet to her, and sat again in his table with Vivian.

"This is the chick of a Phoenix. Isn't it cute? This is the one of the cutest Phoenix chick in our wizards' world, Hank take

care of it very good. I give 20 points to Adventurer Team. The Phoenix chick can also heal wizards. Phoenix is one of the favorite pet in the world", said Miss Dane while Phonnet was warmed by Miss Dane's soft hand.

And she continued, *"Who was wounded here? Velvy, I think you have wounds after scarred by the Griffins in the 'Flyball' game, right?"*, asked Miss Dane, looked at Velvy, one of the 14 years student, and Velvy was going to Miss Dane and Phonnet, hoping she would be healed. 20 seconds later,

Velvy's wound was healed, and she became happy again.

"You looked how it works right in front of your eyes", said Miss Dane while Velvy kissed Phonnet and went back to her seat.

"Phoenixes can bring very heavy loads and they can be used to send letters or daily news to us when they are growing up. I think…Phoenix is the most fantastic myth creature in the world…and I remember…when I was 4, I was healed by my family's Phoenix, and I still remember it now."

The bells rang and Miss Dane said, *"Homework: read more about Phoenix in the library. There are one hundred of it. Time's up!"*, said Miss Dane while she handed Phonnet back to Hank and Vivian.

CHAPTER 9

THE LESSON WITH PROFESSOR VICTOR

Miss Dane smiled at them and Professor Victor came in with a big smile.

"Hello'h everybod'eh! Still remember me'h?", asked Professor Victor.

"Yes, we are, Professor", answered Vivian loudly and everybody laughed.

"Well, we hafta' defence ourselves from the dark magics, right? So'h, it's me'h work! We'h have to skilled the white magic firs', to protect ourselves from the dark magic or the black magic. If yu'h feels a dark magic squeezes yu'h, just say this, your magic word, and 'Perita Protectiva!' D'un't try now ye'h? No'h dark magic, right?", asked Professor Victor.

"*Yeah*", answered Hank and everybody giggled, included Hank.

"*Professor Victor!*", said Vivian suddenly, her sound broke the giggles.

"*I have a feeling when I was 8 years old, I felt that the dark magic squeezed me so tight until I couldn't breathe. But someone came to my place where I was standing, fighting the dark magic, and the dark magic was running so fast and I couldn't see the one who helped me, it looked like my…mom…in the ghost version…*", Vivian finished.

"Oh...", answered Professor Victor, *"I...it was your mum who send'h the white magic! 'Perita Protectiva' spell can be send'h to anybody. Even humans!"*

"I...still remember the day Professor...February the 21th!", said Vivian.

They enjoyed the lesson very much, but not much more than the lesson with Professor McGall. They learnt the most helpful lesson that is very easy with Professor Victor. They seemed to like the hour at this lesson very much, because how helpful it would be to them, and to everyone who needed it, because, all of the white magic could be sent to anybody, even the humans, real humans. Professor Victor had a bad language of English, but who cares? Anybody could know what he meant. It's one of a magic that Professor Victor gave to everybody he met and it stayed forever in your life. Hank told Professor Victor about his case like Vivian's with the dark magic, but, the one who sent it was his dad, and Professor Victor told everybody again that everybody who had something connected to him or her could know the case and sent the white magic to the one who squeezed by the black magic.

CHAPTER 10

THE 'FLYBALL' GAME

The bells rang again and it meant, the hour with Professor Victor was done, the hour of giggles. They always had one hour more to play before the dinner time at 7 o' clock in the evening. But Hank and Vivian had to train the 'Flyball' game with Bugman at 6 o' clock, the time they finished the class. Hank and Vivian searched for Bugman after the class, circling the school, and they met Bugman waiting them in front of the class.

"Well…we miss 10 minutes for training. I think you were still in the class, but…are you circling the school?", asked Bugman.

"Y…yes we are", answered Vivian.

Then, Bugman walked to the 'Flyball' park, followed by Hank and Vivian.

"This, is the park. Let's see what you can! 'Golden Falcon' is thrown up to the sky!", said Bugman clearly while he threw the 'Golden Falcon' to the sky.

Hank and Vivian were now soaring up to the sky, searching for the fantastic Falcon, while Hank and Vivian heard Bugman yelled, *"No magic! No magic!"*.

"Watch out Vivian!", yelled Hank while a griffin pawed Vivian. *"Argh! My shoulder! I have a wound!"*, yelled Vivian painfully.

But then, they were separated, Hank on the right, while Vivian on the left.

Then, Hank saw it, the Falcon, stayed at its place.

"Vivian! Found it! Go here!", yelled Hank loudly.

A girl came to the Falcon, raised her hand, it was Vivian. But the Falcon went near the ground, and a giant spider made Hank falling from his broom.

"Just go! Go Vivian!", said Hank while the spider showed its legs, ready to pounce on Hank, but Vivian came back to Hank, with a medium spikey rock in her hand, and the spikey rock

was thrown to the spider's stomach, and the spider was dead.

"I will not lose a second when my friend is hurt. Look at your wound! It's big enough!", said Vivian.

The 'Golden Falcon' showed itself again near Vivian's wounded shoulder, and Vivian catched it! On the ground!

"Great! I don't think you two can do it! I will grant you 10 points each of you! Very great!", yelled Bugman from far away, and running to them.

"Thanks", said Hank, handed the 'Golden Falcon' from Vivian's hand to Bugman.

"Well…you two better go off to the 'Feast Place', but better take a bath first and rest for minutes. It's still 15 minutes before the dinner. This first training is very great! You please can come to the match a week later! Your opponents are Harm Team, Love Team, and Healer Team. Remember to use magic only if it's emergency.", said Bugman.

"HARM TEAM!", yelled Hank and Vivian very loudly until Bugman looked very shocked.

"What's wrong with...", asked Bugman, but stopped by Hank, giving codes to Bugman that they wanted to be killed and Phonnet wanted to be harmed by Harm Team in Professor McGall's lesson.

"I want to say then... Harms Team's members was Gillbert Dracort, called Dracort, and Dulcia Vampirte, called Vampirte, and Dracort's Griffin, Cedric, and Vampirte's Phoenix, Flaret. Their pet were same gender with their owners", whispered Bugman.

"Well…thanks then, for the information, Mr. Bugman. We will do what you say and…we will train by ourselves.

Thanks", added Hank quickly before Bugman said the words again, "*I trusted you that Adventurers Team will win, and you will be healed in the Wounded Wing, and someone will heal your wounds."*

CHAPTER 11

THE TALKS ABOUT THE SAME DREAM

They quickly went to the Wounded Wing, and their wounds were healed now permanently by an old but pretty woman called Madam Treta. They were running to their house, and took a bath there, and rested for 5 minutes and went to the 'Feast Place'.

"I want to talk to you, Hank", said Vivian after they had their foods on their plate.

"About a dream?", asked Hank.

"Yes…I dreamed we were wounded like we were in the Wounded Wing, and, we were wounded because the'Flyball' game…someone made that dream for us", answered Vivian.

"Omigosh! My dream was about that too! But…I know who make that dream

to us...Professor Noricked! He seemed that he didn't want us to play the 'Flyball' game. Other teachers will say yes with that popular game, but he won't!", said Hank seriously.

"I think so...anybody will be proud when their children or students can be one of the participants of the 'Flyball' game, and they can even cancel the lesson for him or her!", said Vivian.

"Yes, you are right", answered Hank. *"But if Professor Noricked was trying to make us not to be one of the participants of the 'Flyball', why?"*, asked Vivian.

"I think…there is something hiding from Professor Noricked's heart…but don't be that suspicious. Maybe he is just jealous because he didn't…but anyway…the dream was true, right? And, maybe…we were just too thinking about the Flyball", Hank answered.

"Yes, sorry Hank. I was a very suspicions girl…don't worry", said Vivian.

They finished their dinner, and walked in the night, circling the school, still talking about Professor Noricked and talking about the other teachers that were very kind to them. They went back in to their house, and finished their homework, after met Dracort, Vampirte, Cedric, and Flaret.

"Well here's the boy and the girl, in the night, trying to be the detective? ...HAHAHAHAHH!", said Vampirte with her jealous and hoarse voice, followed by their thundering laughter, even their pets and even Flaret, a Phoenix, laughed too.

Dracort was wearing a blue robe, with his lemonade skin, and his tidy shining hair, and Vampirte was wearing a turqouise robe, and her lemonade skin, and her long, smooth hair made her look more precious, but it's not because of her jealous face. Hank and Vivian ignored them. They just got in to their house, and locked the door.

"That boy and girl make me feel sick", said Vivian.

Hank just stroked Phonnet's warming body to make himself not angry.

CHAPTER 12

THE 'FLYBALL' MATCH

One week later and it was the day Phonnet grew bigger than before, and Miss Dane couldn't stop to say how good was Phonnet's growth when it's on her lesson. One day, it was night, and heard flaps of wings. Every student, who was now in the 'Feast Place', eating their dinner, became very silent, and trying to hear more about the flaps of wings. Then, heard a boy, screaming, and the scream heard in one second. The scream heard from Hank's left, and all students with the teachers went to the left, and found a boy from Dragon Team was fainted with wounds on his two little shoulders, and the boy was now carried to the Wounded Wing.

"It looks like the scars of a Dragon", said a girl.

"No…it looks like the bites of serpent, but it's not…wings…flaps of wings…", said her friend.

Professor McGall went straight to the Adventurer Team, and said, *"I hope, no one will be fainted again, Adventurer Team"*

"We hope so", answered Vivian.

The day for the 'Flyball' match was coming, Hank and Vivian, with Phonnet on Hank's shoulder, were ready in front of the empty gate to get in to the 'Flyball' park. The gates were 4, each gate for one team. The gate was opened, and every team member of this 'Flyball' match was now soaring up to the sky, and hearing Bugman said, *"The animals and the 'Golden Falcon' were released! Game starts!"*.

The Falcon was now disappeared to the golden sun, and Hank with Vivian split into two searching the Falcon, while students below them were cheering. Suddenly, Hank and Vivian, both at the same time, were now facing the Griffin, and they were now starting to fight it. Phonnet was helping Hank to fight the Griffin until the Griffin was now blinded by her, and started to blind the Griffin that Vivian was facing. The Griffins that was attacking Hank and Vivian were now blinded, and fell to the ground, and Hank and Vivian went into one group again, because Vivian was led by Phonnet to Hank and specially, Hank saw the Falcon near the ground, resting. They dove to the ground, and the Falcon was still resting there, and there's no spiders.

Hank tried to catch it without sounds, and… *"Hank get the Falcon! Adventurer Team…wins!!!"*, yelled Bugman very loudly. Hank handed the Falcon to

Bugman, and the Falcon's fantastic wings was getting no energy.

"The bonus is to get 50 points. Congratulations!", said Bugman.

CHAPTER 13

THE ATTACKS

The attacks were getting often now in only one week, and this was making Hank so suspicious about the animal who was attacking the students. One night, Vivian founded a trapdoor in their bedroom, and they opened the key by magic, and found only the darkness.

"*Maybe we need our wand to light the darkness?*", asked Hank.

"*Yes, we are. 'Hocus Pocus! Listera!'*", answered Vivian, and light was coming from Vivian's wand, and Hank said the spell too.

"*I think, we must be an animal, so, we can't be known if the culprit was a human*", said Vivian.

"*We have to be an animal because we want to be faster. Be a bird, Vivian!*", said Hank while he took his 'Animal Transformer' potion.

Vivian did the same with Hank, and the two drank it one gulp, and *said "Peregrine Falcon!"*, and the two became the fastest animal in the world. Phonnet was now flying, leading them, but Hank and Vivian were faster than her. They dove down to the dark, and they hit the ground, where the darkness was ended, and there was a big cave, looked like a home for a myth creature that lived together in one pack.

"*I…*", said Hank, stopped, because he saw a claw that looked like it was belonged to a Scobat, a medium myth creature that was a mix of a scorpion and a bat. Its scorpion tail could be turned like an owl's head, even could still be turned more than an owl, and could stop in any position. Its scorpion feet could make them landing anywhere. Their fangs of a bat were poisonous, could kill 3 men because of its big mouth. Their body of a bat and their powerful bat wings could sweep 10 men at one time.

Their claws could make the one who was gripped by their claws fainted.

"This was like a Scobat's claw, but...who released the Scobats?", asked Vivian while Hank took the claw from the ground with his beak.

They were shocked when they saw Professor Noricked was there, talking to the Scobats with their language, and Hank and Vivian thought they were talking about their invasion to the wizards' world to defeat anybody who was mastered at magic wand, because, Professor Noricked wanted to be the best, and he was angry to the Scobats, because they didn't kill the boy at the first attack and the others who were mastered at magic wand that were attacked.

"How dare you! Why you didn't kill the boy and the others! Why…you just a rubbish!", said Professor Noricked in Scobats' language.

"I think, we just let Professor Noricked go out from this cave, and then, we kill the Scobats first", said Hank.

"No, Hank, we will be dead…there are 5 Scobats", answered Vivian.

Professor Noricked got out from that cave, but didn't see Phonnet, and Hank with Vivian in Peregrine Falcon version.

"Now, let's fight. Give this to Phonnet first", whispered Hank.

Vivian just narrowed her eyes while Phonnet would blind the Scobats. But, when Phonnet blinded the last Scobat, Phonnet was dead.

"Phonnet!", yelled Hank in Falcon's voice while Phonnet breathed for the last time.

CHAPTER 14

THE FIGHTING WITH SCOBATS AND THE SECRETS

"*Turningwizz!*", said Hank and Vivian together. Vivian went running to Phonnet, trying all spells to make

Phonnet rise again while Hank seemed to be fainted and about to cry.

"*Aaaaaah!*", shrieked Vivian.

Hank woke up again from the fainted feelings. Fire licked the top of the cave, but the cave didn't burn. Then, came a young Phoenix, soaring up to the sky and landed on Hank's shoulder.

"*Phonnet...*", said Hank breathlessly.

But then, Phonnet flew up again, clawed the scorpion tail of all the Scobats there, and their tail now wasn't poisonous anymore.

Phoenixes were a myth creature who had shield of poison and their claws could make the poisons gone from a creature's body.

"*'Hocus Pocus, Hitselanders!'*", yelled Vivian, pointed her wand to their claws, and their claws were broken now, and Hank yelled, "*'Hocus Pocus, Hitselanders!'*", and one Scobat was hit right in the middle of its stomach, and the Scobat was fainted.

Phonnet was now bitting its neck to kill it.

"'*Hocus Pocus, Hitselanders!*'", said Vivian, did the same with Hank, pointed her wand to the middle of its stomach, and the Scobat was fainted again.

Phonnet kept doing her work, biting the Scobats' neck until the Scobats were dead. After all of the Scobats were dead, Professor Noricked came in, and said, "*Omigosh!*", looked at the Scobats.

"*How dare you!*", continued him.

Without saying anything, Vivian and Hank drank one gulp and became a

Peregrine Falcon, and Hank, Vivian, and Phonnet flew up from the light back to their bedroom. They locked the trapdoor again so tight until no one could open it, even with magic. It was morning on Saturday, and was holiday time until Sunday.

They ran to the Teachers' Office, and saw that Professor McGall would get out, and said in panic, *"Professor, please, you should follow us, please…"*

"Whoa, whoa, please. I will follow you if you are not panicked. Easy", answered Professor McGall calmly.

They went to Hank and Vivian's bedroom, and showed Professor McGall the trapdoor. Vivian suggested Professor McGall to be a bird, and these birds, (Hank, Vivian, and Professor McGall without Phonnet), were diving to the light. They bumped again to the ground, and transformed back into themselves with their magic wands gripped tightly in front of them. Professor McGall looked shocked when he saw the dead Scobats, and Professor Noricked there. They became wizards again to speak.

"Noricked! What are you doing here?", asked Professor McGall confusedly.

"Oh…I…I…" "He is the one who trained this dead Scobats, that previous hour ago were still alive, and killed the masters of magic wand!", answered Hank furiously.

"Kid!", yelled Professor Noricked in panic.

"Noricked! You will have this detention! You will be a prisoner for 20 years or until you realize what you are doing!", answered Professor McGall furiously with his shining green eyes glittering.

They took the potion again to became a bird, and went back to Hank and Vivian's bedroom, being wizards again. They locked the trapdoor, so, Professor Noricked's prison was there.

"*Professor, you should thank to Phonnet. She many times helped us to fight, and she was dead once for us when she blinded the Scobats.*

"*I…thank her, Professor*", said Hank firmly.

"*I thank to all of you. You receive…*"

"*Stop Professor!*", yelled Hank and Vivian.

"*We can't receive the points. Any students can do this if they see the trapdoor*", said Hank and Vivian both and together.

"*Ok, then. Thanks for helping to solve this mystery*", continued Professor McGall.

CHAPTER 15

THE NEW MEMBER OF ADVENTURER TEAM

On Monday morning, when they took the breakfast together in the 'Feast Place', Professor Ganag said to all students in the 'Feast Place', that the mystery was solved by

Hank, Vivian, and Phonnet. They became red, and Professor McGall told them to get in front of all the students. They were told by Professor Ganag to sit again, and continued their breakfast. Harm Team was envier now, and they felt they wanted to harm Hank, Vivian, and Phonnet.

But in Friday afternoon, after all the class was finished, Vivian said, *"Hank, I have to rush to go there. I saw an egg falling from that tree! I have to rescue it now!"*, said Vivian, running to the egg's place in the bushes.

A minute later, Vivian was coming back, with an egg in her hand.

"Wow, Vivian. You caught a Phoenix's egg. That's yours", said Hank walking to their house for some rest and bath. Vivian got the egg to her pocket, and walked following Hank to their house.

When they arrived at their home, they took a bath, and Vivian's egg was cracked, and a Phoenix chick was coming out by himself.

"Oh! He's very cute!", said Vivian, trying to hold her sobs and tears of happiness.

"Congratulations, Vivian! It's a Phoenix egg. His mother was searching for food, but this egg was falling from the nest. It's only a minute before it hatched, and you take care of it now, Vivian", said Hank while he walked to the male bathroom in their house.

Vivian asked Phonnet to guard Treckno, her Phoenix chick while she took a bath, and Phonnet said yes. They took a bath, and went to the 'Feast Place', bringing their new-joiner, the male Phoenix that Vivian named Treckno, to Professor Ganag, who was sitting there, waiting for students to come there to eat their dinner.

"Well, just take care of Treckno, and he will be your great Phoenix, Vivian", said Professor Ganag.

Professor Ganag was proud Vivian got a pet, and then, the bells rang, and all the students ran there to the 'Feast Place', but Team Harm was sneaking while Professor Ganag speaked to Hank and Vivian, and they became envier and envier.

"I…really want to harm them…really", said Dracort, and answered by Vampirte, "Me too".

Treckno, who was still a chick, was taken care by Vivian so good that Miss Dane was very proud with Vivian too.

CHAPTER 16

ANOTHER MYSTERY

Miss Dane looked very happy, and she was walking towards Hank and Vivian.

"Thanks! You two make me a Professor because I was teaching you and the others properly with Phoenixes that belong to *you! I can't do this without you!"*, said Professor Dane, hugged them.

"Well, congratulations, then", said Vivian happily.

"I give you 20 points. Treckno and Phonnet are the best Phoenixes I've ever seen!", continued Professor Dane.

Phonnet was landing on Professor Dane's shoulder, and Treckno, who was now a Phoenix kid, was landing to the ground, bowing to Professor Dane. The next day, Professor Dane told the class that now, she was a Professor, and she was helped by Hank and Vivian. Hank and Vivian became red again. They caught Dracort and Vampirte's jealous and furious eye. They seemed to harm Hank and Vivian now, and they did!

"'*Alakazam*! *Hitselanders!*' ", yelled Dracort and Vampirte together, pointed their wand to Hank and Vivian, and Hank, together with Vivian, got wounds now.

Professor Dane was giving them detention and missed 40 points for Harm Team, and Phonnet and Treckno healed them both.

"Are you ok?", asked Professor Dane softly.

"Yes...we are fine...don't worry", answered Vivian after healed.

At night, no one knew what was it, but all students heard hisses when they would go to bed. The hiss was soft, but sounded scary. Hank and Vivian discussed this all night, and they thought that this monster had grown by someone. They were suspicious with Professor Noricked, and they really thought it was Professor Noricked's work. They had break 2 hours now because Professor

Noricked didn't teach anymore, but they were still suspicious about him. They taught it was a serpent, but they heard a floating sound, and they still confused about this unsolved mystery.

One night, they heard this hissing sounds again, but this wasn't really a snake. In one week, all students had to stay in their house, because, this hissing sound was now heard in the daylight too, except for eating, they would hurry go to the 'Feast Place'.

At last, all of the students would not come out even in emergency things, except, for breakfast, lunch, and dinner.

Hank and Vivian were sad about this, but they didn't give up to find the culprit. They became birds again one morning, and came down to Professor Noricked's prison.

Phonnet and Treckno were the same age, young after they burned themselves 1 month ago. Phoenixes could burn themselves if they felt they were old enough or if they wanted to start a new life.

CHAPTER 17

THE FIGHTING PART 2

They went down, with Phonnet and Treckno. Hank and Vivian got Professor Noricked saving 3 eggs, and Professor Noricked was sitting on a chair, guarding his eggs.

"Vivian! I have read a guide of the eggs book! It was an Invisible Dragon egg! They can go straight through the walls and they are like serpents!", whispered Hank.

"I've read it this Dragon was not invisible, but invisible if they go straight through the walls and anything", whispered Vivian trying to remember something else.

They soared up again, and became a wizard and witch again. *"So...Professor Noricked got that eggs from...?"*, asked Vivian.

"I think, he found it somewhere...no! It's not like that! I have seen he had that eggs when we fought the Scobats!", answered Hank.

One month passed, and they were eating the dinner. They walked back to their house after dinner and the Bird Team founded a girl fainted there, and the teachers together brought her to the Wounded Wing. The girl was Vampirte, looked shocked. Dracort's silent tears were pouring down from his eyes, and he got in to his house that was not far from Hank and Vivian's.

"I've heared that the Invisible Dragon's body, which can go straight to anything, can make a person fainted if the dragon flies towards him or her", said Vivian.

"We have to be an adventurer now, start from tonight", said Hank darkly while he went to his house with Vivian.

That night, they went down again to the prison as a bird, and Phonnet with Treckno were following now. They watched that the Dragons were now young dragons, because they drank the speeding up growth potion from Professor Noricked, ready to kill or make terrors again.

"Now! You have to make terrors to this school. Make the Magic Wand Masters killed or terrored, because, I want to be a magic Wand Master too! HAHAHAHAHAHA HAHAHAHAH!", his laugh thundering and the dragons started to walk to the trapdoor, and disappeared.

The Adventurer Team were chasing them all the night, but they kept thudding to things. The Dragons got in to the Bird Team's house, made them fainted, and went to another house.

"'*Turningwizz!*'", said Hank and Vivian, and they said together,

"'*Hocus Pocus, Hitselanders!*'", and one Dragon was fainted with wounds, and Treckno went to the Dragon to bite its neck, and the Dragon was dead.

They were in front of the Teacher's Bedroom now, and they took their potion again, and got in to the trapdoor again, tried not to wake up the teachers. Professor Noricked had gone to bed, and the Dragons following him. Hank said after transforming into wizard again,

"'*Hocus Pocus!*' *Hitselanders!*'", and Vivian followed Hank by pointing her wand to another Dragon.

"What's going on here?", said Professor Noricked.

"You! Get away from here! Dragons! Attack!", shouted Professor Noricked.

Hank, Vivian, Phonnet, and Treckno, were fighting with them, trying not to get hit. After all the Dragons were dead with the same spell, another creature coming, a very giant spider.

"How do you feel now? Don't give up? Attack!", yelled Professor Noricked.

The giant spider moved, and one of its feet was standing on Hank, who was lying spread-eagled on the cave floor.

"*Hank!*", shouted Vivian.

"*Just…fight…the…*", and Hank fainted before he finished his sentence.

Treckno was biting one of its leg, and the leg was cracked because of Treckno! While Phonnet hitting its eyes.

"'*Hocus Pocus!*' *Hitselanders!*'", yelled Vivian.

The Spider was hit 30% and came to Vivian blindly because Phonnet hit its eyes. Phoenixes could revive people, so, Phonnet was reviving Hank, who was fainted. Hank opened his eyes, and saw Vivian was in trouble, and yelled powerfully,

"'Hocus Pocus!' Hitselanders!". The spider was hit 40%, and it became very angry and started to bump anywhere blindly.

"Vivian! Watch out!", yelled Hank when Vivian would be bumped by the spider in 3 seconds.

"Thanks!", yelled Vivian back.

They yelled together while the Phoenixes kept hitting the spider ferociously, *"'Hocus Pocus!* 'Hitselanders!'".

A blinding light came from Hank and Vivian's wand, and when the light touched the spider, the spider exploded.

"Wha...?", asked Professor Noricked breathlessly without finishing his sentence.

CHAPTER 18

THE FIGHTING WITH PROFESSOR NORICKED

"You crushed my dear spider!", said Professor Noricked with his eyes popping out.

"We have to", said Hank.

"Well, said goodbye to your life", said Professor Noricked, pointed his wand on Vivian.

But Treckno came and took Professor Noricked's wand, and threw it from the highest place in the cave.

"Look? My wand isn't broken, right? It's high quality and can kill anybody", said Professor Noricked.

Professor Noricked's body was turned to a serpent, ready to fight. It's not only a serpent, it's much bigger than the spider until it crashed the upper of the cave.

"RUN! RUN!", yelled Vivian.

They had turned into birds, ready to fly, but Professor Noricked, the Giant Serpent, was bitting their tail, and Hank with Vivian transformed into wizard and witches again.

"*What do you want, Noricked?*", asked Hank bravely.

Then, heard an echoing hissing sound, "*I want to kill anybody who stopped my task: killing all Magic Wand Masters. Although you two are the Master of Myth Creatures, you want to stop my work. So, this is the detention from me*" "What do you want from us, *old snake? You can't take anything from us!"*, said Vivian and looked at the Phoenixes, Phonnet and Treckno.

The Giant Serpent looked at the Phoenixes too, and said, *"You still have to fight me first, adventurers"*, his Serpent face came nearer and nearer to their faces.

He hissed, and ready to strike them, but these clever students said, *"'Hocus Pocus!' 'Bobbleprotecta!'"* But he was too strong.

He cracked the bubbles, and they were unprotected now. Phonnet and Treckno started to sing their song, which could add the brave feelings and added the instinct of a pure hearted wizard.

"'Hocus Pocus!' 'Hitselanders!", said Hank and Vivian together again, and the same blinding light came out from their wands and hit the Giant Serpent right on his head.

The Giant Serpent's eye was blinded, and his eye's blood was spreading to hank and Vivian, making their robes red. He bumped anywhere and started to crash the cave. It was morning now. Hank and Vivian, together with Phonnet and Treckno, fighting the Giant Serpent with anything they could, and for the final, "'*Hocus Pocus*!' '*Hitselanders*!'", said Hank and Vivian together, and the light came out again, giving the very super hitting points for anything.

The Giant Serpent was dead, and Hank got healed by Phonnet. Vivian's wounds got healed by Treckno. The birds (Hank, Vivian, Phonnet, and Treckno), were back in the bedroom, locked the trapdoor so tight, and went to the 'Feast Place' without taking a bath, and with bloods of the Giant Serpent's eye.

CHAPTER 19

THE TRUTH

They were looked very tired. They were very tired. They seemed to be fainted. Before Hank and Vivian reached the 'Feast Place's floor, they fell and fainted. Phonnet and Treckno went to Professor Victor, and all students were going to the place where Hank and Vivian fainted. One hour later, when they opened their eyes, they heard all of the students were waiting in front of the Wounded Wing's door. They sat up, and Professor Victor with the previous wounded and fainted students that Hank and Vivian had rescued, by solving the mystery, came in and sat on some chairs that were near to their twin beds.

"Tell me'h the truth", asked Professor Victor kindly, but forgot to ask if Hank and Vivian felt ok.

Hank and Vivian told the truth that Professor Noricked was a bad man. They attacked some fierce myth creatures. About Professor Noricked being a Giant Serpent, and another story.

At last, Professor Victor said, *"Let's go down'h then. Show me'h the Serpent"* When they got out from the Wounded Wing, many students gasped because of Hank and Vivian Giant Serpent's blood, which still stick on their robes, but Hank and Vivian didn't care and didn't noticed.

They went down again as birds, and became wizards again, and Professor Victor saw the Giant Serpent and the myth creatures that were death.

"This is the truth. We can't sleep for all night", said Vivian.

"Yes...we heard sounds from the trapdoor last night", said Hank.

Professor Victor examined the Giant Serpent's body, and there was silence for 5 minutes.

At last, Professor Victor said, *"Thanks for helping us. We think you were gone previous night when we will breakfast. I think this school have to be'h closed. Thanks"*, said Professor Victor.

"Yeah, thanks, too", answered Hank.

They went up again and after became wizards and witch again, Professor Victor said, *"I am suspicious with Professor Noricked yu'h know'h. At last, these 4 heroes came to this school and rescued us all. Thanks."*

Hank and Vivian just said, *"We will take the breakfast now."*

They walked to the 'Feast Place' and founded the teachers were pale, waiting for the story.

"Victor, what...?", asked Professor Ganag.

"I will tell yu'h all at breakfast, and will showed you the truth", answered Professor Victor.

CHAPTER 20

THE CELEBRATION AND THE QUESTIONS

"*Hank and Vivian! What are you doing?*", asked a boy, looking up and down to their robes.

"Eh? ... Just see with the teachers", answered Vivian, grinning.

They felt very hungry and they ate until full. The teachers went to the trapdoor, followed by the students.

"This is the place", said Professor Victor to the birds (the teachers and the students).

Everybody became wizards again, and gasped. Phonnet and Treckno were following them, showed all the rooms of the cave.

"Well, I think Professor Noricked had a private room because he never slept with us from the start", said Professor Dane.

"You are right", answered Miss Miserandusy.

"Maybe we have to add them points?", asked Bugman.

"They will not want to have it", said professor McGall.

The students thought hard that only four persons could kill this all. Harm Team was felt envier, envier and envier. But they were embarrassed too, because Vampirte had been rescued by Adventurer Team.

The students gave questions to Hank and Vivian, and after many many students asked, at last, they told them the story.

Hank and Vivian were telling the truth in one hour, after they finished the breakfast. The questions on each other became more various, and Hank with Vivian and the Phoenixes started learning again this day. This was Pofessor Ganag's lesson, with all of the students in this school.

"Let's say congratulations to Hank, Vivian, Phonnet, and Treckno! If they were not here, this school would be closed. All of the students, have to go to another school if this school closed", said Professor Ganag.

All students were afraid with the look of the Giant Serpent's blood on Hank and Vivian's robes. They learned the poison potion, which could kill the 4 fierce Dragons at one time. At the feast, Hank, Vivian, and Phonnet were celebrated again and Harm Team was willing to battle their pets. The envy feeling of Harm Team was now uncontrollable. They were willing to fight just because the Giant Serpent that finished by Hank, Vivian, Treckno, and Phonnet.

What an alarming situation of Harm Team's envy feeling that was on their black hearts. From their team's name, everybody knew that their hearts were already black, event their pets and even their Phoenixes!

CHAPTER 21

THE BATTLE

The next day, Dracort was having Hank to battle their pets. Phonnet and Treckno knew that because Phoenixes could. Cedric, Flaret, Phonnet, and Treckno were waiting for the night, to fight. At the midnight, Hank, Vivian, Dracort, and Vampirte were having their pets, and went out to the land out the school to battle their pets.

Phonnet and Treckno were standing like a statue, very calm and patient. Cedric and Flaret started to fight, but Flaret became frozen, because Treckno, Vivian's male Phoenix, hypnotized Flaret to freeze by his male eye calmly. Flaret was soaring up to the sky, soaring up and up, and gone.

"You! What are you doing to my Phoenix!", said Vampirte coldly to

Treckno with her eye widened and her forehead wrinkled.

Phonnet and Treckno let Cedric smashed and hit them, while Hank and Vivian were having silent tears. Treckno and Phonnet were dead, and Dracort shrieked happily to Phonnet and Treckno, "HAHAHA! WHAT ARE YOU DOING, FOOL? GET UP! GET UP!"

"*You lose, Hank and Vivian*", said Vampirte darkly.

But Hank and Vivian stayed calm, and their tears wiped out. Dracort's Griffin, Cedric looked very exhausted. Dracort, Vampirte, Cedric, without Flaret were going back to the school, when fire licked the sky.

"What the…", asked Dracort with his eyes widened.

Dracort and Vampirte forgot that Phoenixes could be reborn to the same age if they were dead in the battle, and could burn themselves to the baby age.

Phonnet and Treckno were reborned, and fighting Cedric, and Cedric was dead. Dracort and Vampirte's body were like the boneless men, and went back to their bedroom sadly. Hank and Vivian went to bed too, with their pajamas set.

"What a good battle, they are forgetting all about Phoenixes!", said Hank happily from his bed to Phonnet and Treckno.

Treckno flew to Vivian's sheet, and slept there. Phonnet was standing on Hank's sheet, who was sleeping. Phonnet sit down, and fell asleep, exhausted too. The next morning would be another story.

CHAPTER 22

THE PURE ANIMTRA

On Professor Victor's lesson, he said that Professor Noricked's how to see your future lesson, would be changed into the History of Magic lesson by a new teacher.

The next day, Professor Ganag, who looked ferocious lately before this day, was now became a healthy-looking woman and always smiled.

She even would tell a story of the history of magic and the other stories on her lesson. She was very proud of Hank, Vivian, and Phonnet. This day, she told the class about the Animtra. Hank and Vivian, the book lovers, were trying to remember the book they had read together about the Animtra.

On the lunch time, Hank and Vivian were eating slowly, trying hard to remember the book from the library about Animtra.

Just then after their silence for 10 minutes, Hank said to Vivian and looked on her face, *"Vivian, I remember…"*, said Hank but stopped because of the appearance of Vivian on the table and she also recognized that Hank was an eagle, sitting on the table.

"Hank…we are the Animtra", said Vivian.

Each Animtra could know the speaking of other Animtra in the animal appearance, even though they were in different species. Every Animtra would change into an animal that they really loved at the first time they became the Animtra, and back into wizard form after saying '*Turningwizz*' in their head.

Fortunately, there were no students or teachers anymore in the 'Feast Place'. Hank and Vivian were back into wizard form again, with Phonnet and Treckno widened their eyes in front of them.

Hank and Vivian continued eating, and back to their bedroom. They couldn't believe what happened, and went asleep. The Animtras could do the transformation to animal every time they wanted and could change into wizard or witch form again anytime.

The next day, Hank and Vivian told Professor Ganag that Dracort and Vampirte made Adventurer Team fighting their pets with theirs.

Dracort and Vampirte were having their detention to help Madam Tretta scrubbing the beds in the Wounded Wing. Vivian told Professor Victor after his lesson quietly that Hank and Vivian had the Animtra power and begged his help not to tell anybody about Hank and Vivian's power.

Harm Team was trying to hit Hank, Vivian, Phonnet, and Treckno again, so, Hank and Vivian must turn into an eagle and a cat for two hours after the lessons. Dracort and Vampirte were very angry to the Adventurer Team, and don't know about the Animtra.

"Where are Hank and Vivian?", said Dracort angrily with his wand ready.

Vampirte caught the eye of Treckno and Phonnet, but didn't see the cat and the eagle, which were Vivian and Hank. Treckno and Phonnet gripped Vampirte's wand, and soaring high and high, and with a crash, the wand was landed on the ground and broken. Treckno had given the information that Vampirte had two wands to Phonnet.

"My wand! How did you know about this, Phonnet and Treckno?", asked Vampirte, eye widened.

"Be thankful it's not your neck, Vampirte", said Vivian softly.

"How did you come here? I didn't see you!", asked Dracort loudly.

They were talking in the 'Flyball' park. Phonnet and Treckno flew to

Hank and Vivian's shoulder, and they walked togeteher to their house.

"*Good idea, Treckno. You saw Vampirte's another wand. Thanks to you too*", said Vivian to Treckno and pointed at Phonnet.

Phonnet just bowed her head.

CHAPTER 23

THE LAST NIGHT IN THE YEAR AND THE RETURN TO HOME

Hank's and Vivian's robes were still a little bit red, because of the Giant Serpent's blood.

At the night feast, Professor Ganag was celebrating Hank, Vivian, Treckno, and Phonnet again for helping the school.

All of the children were happy there, except Dracort and Vampirte without pets. The next year, of course, would be greater, but of course more difficult about the lessons.

Hank and Vivian kept their secret of their power of the pure Animtra, that was really special. Professor Victor was keeping the secret too, and kept a look to Hank and Vivian with their Phoenixes.

"I hope, it is a nice holiday for all, and next year, I hope, greater", said Professor Dane in the 'Feast Place'.

She looked at Hank, who helped her to be a professor. Hank and Vivian were enjoying the school, and enjoying Professor Victor's lesson, and, of course, the 'Flyball'.

The next day, all children would go back to their home without a train, because it's the tradition. Hank and Vivian were having their badge of 'The Champion of the School', and went flew to their home. At the middle of the route to home, Vivian's trunk was crashed to the land, and her diary book broke into two.

"Oh my! What an unlucky day!", said Vivian sadly after Hank and Vivian landed.

"Be thankful it's not your neck, Vivian", said Hank.

Vivian and Hank, together with Phonnet and Treckno laughed together.

They finally reached home, after two hours. Their mom and dad looked shock with Hank and Vivian's "red" robes.

"*What are you doing?*", asked Vivian's dad to both of them.

Hank and Vivian was twinkling their eyes at each other and at the Phoenixes.

Just then, their mom and dad looked at the shining brand-new badge. Hank and Vivian went back to Hank's tree house and discussed about their success in killing that filthy Giant Serpent.

Vivian was having Hank's family to have dinner at her house, told their moms and dads about all the story at school. It's time for dinner, Hank and Vivian told their mom and dad about the Giant Serpent and Dracort and Vampirte. This year was a very special first year at the School of Wizardry for the "Friol" (Hank, Vivian, Phonnet, and Treckno). The two families had also received the thank you mail from the school to Hank and Vivian. Great for the "Friol".

THE END

© 2017 Anna Margaret Yohan

Terms and Conditions:

The purchaser of this book (paperback or ebook) is subject to the condition that he/she shall in no way resell it, nor any part of it, nor make copies of it to distribute freely.

All Persons Fictitious Disclaimer:

This book is a work of fiction. Any similarity between the characters and situations within its pages and places or persons, living or dead, is unintentional and co-incidental.

ABOUT THE AUTHOR

Anna Margaret Yohan is a young writer from Jakarta, Indonesia. Born in 2008, Anna started to write books since age 9. She loves writing detective, mystery, and adventure stories. Famous authors such as J. K. Rowling and Elisabetta Dami have been her inspiration in writing books. She enjoys reading fiction and nonfiction books.

Printed in Great Britain
by Amazon